ONCE UPON A TIME IN GHANA

GHANA EDITION

Traditional Ewe Stories
Retold in English

Anna Cottrell
Agbotadua Togbi Kumassah

Afram Publications (Ghana) Limited

This edition of *Once Upon a Time* is published by

Afram Publications (Ghana) Limited
P.O. Box M 18
Accra, Ghana.
Tel: +233 302 412 561, +233 244 314 103
E-mail: sales@aframpubghana.com
                publishing@aframpubghana.com
Website: www.aframpubghana.com

ISBN: 978 9964701 536

FOREWORD

Once upon a time, in a beautiful land, where battles had been fought and victories won, where life had been lived and wisdom gained, there lived a great people. They created wonderful stories which carried their history and their wisdom and their wit. Stories carried the life blood of the society. Children could not wait for story time! The youth were fired up to carry on the legacies of the great people and cut new paths towards a bright future.

But seasons came and seasons went. Some seasons brought woe and confusion. Some brought powerful strangers whom this great people had never met. The great people began to look at the strangers and then at themselves. "Perhaps we are not such a great people after all," they murmured among themselves. "Maybe our own stories are not so wonderful after all." In this mood, they stopped talking about battles which had been fought and victories won or life that had been lived and wisdom gained.

Children grew into youth and knew very little about their own stories. This great people had almost forgotten their stories because the stories were not alive in the minds and imaginations of their youth and children.

One day, a stranger came to the beautiful land. She worked with the children to help them learn about the big wide world. She was full of curiosity. Who were these people? Why did their children know so little about how life had been lived and wisdom gained? Because she knew the stories of her own people, she was sure that there were many wonderful stories which would bring a spring into the step of the youth and greater understanding among all the people of the big wide world. "Tell me a story! Please tell me a story!" She asked the Leaders and Elders. I want to help to bring your stories back to life and life back into your stories.

The Leaders and Elders had been watching her, how she lived in their community, how she cared for their children. Her message was so simple and yet so deep. She had told the truth. Where were the wit, wisdom and the legacies? And the youth were not fired up to carry on the legacies of the great people. They could only see new paths towards a future far away from the beautiful land.

So the Leaders went to their best storytellers and said: "We are letting the stories of our lives, our wit and our wisdom slip through our fingers." This is all the story tellers needed. This was all the singers, rattle and gong players needed! They had been waiting for the moment to pour out the treasure they had learnt from their own elders many, many, years ago!

The children and youth together with the Chiefs and the Stranger, gathered to hear about Ayiyi the Wily Spider, the animals of the wild, the hunter, the chief and the princess.

The People of the Beautiful Land began to feel once more that they were a great people and that their stories could guide them into the future. The stranger said, "How the big wide world needs to hear from your own stories just what a Great People you are! Your wisdom and wit will win the hearts of many around the world.

And so it is that the stories in the series "Once Upon A Time In Ghana" have been generously shared by the people of Anyako, Dzelukope, Have, Klikor. What a gift! Long may their tongues be oiled and long may our ears be greased.

Esi Sutherland-Addy (Professor)
May 2013

Recorded on location in the Volta Region in Ghana in 2006-7 , these stories are the result of collaboration between Anna Cottrell and Agbotadua Togbi Kumassah. Agbotadua Kumassah translated the Ewe stories into English and Anna Cottrell retold them in contemporary English to give them a wider appeal to the European market where the original selection of the 24 stories were published and distributed under the title "Once Upon a Time in Ghana."

All proceeds from the sale of the original book and also from the sale of this edition in Ghana are destined for the storytellers and their communities in the form of projects which are designed to improve their standard of living.

For further information, visit
www.ghanastorytelling.com

Chapter 1

ATSU, ATSUTSE AND THE WASP

Storyteller: Listen to the story
Audience: So let the story begin
Storyteller: The story falls upon Atsu
Audience: It falls upon Atsu
Storyteller: The story falls upon Atsutse
Audience: It falls upon Atsutse
Storyteller: The story falls upon the Wasp
Audience: It falls upon the Wasp

Storyteller

Once upon a terrible time there was a great famine in the land where Atsu and Atsutse lived. Those who were strong hung on to life by the most fragile of threads, not speaking, not moving for fear of wasting even the smallest drop of energy. As time went on and man and beast grew ever more desperate, they dragged themselves to the only tree known to be surviving the drought which had already devastated all other plants. By great good fortune this tree happened to be a fruit tree, and so all those who managed to reach its protective arms were able to sustain themselves until such time as the rains returned.

You will not be surprised to know that among those who looked to the fruit tree for life at this terrible time was Wasp, who was able to suck the heart out of all the fruit before he dropped the remains onto the ground beneath the tree. Never a popular creature, Wasp was now even more loathed and despised as his bullying ways became ever more apparent. Foremost amongst those who scorned him was his mother-in-law, who taunted him for his puny body and for his lack of friends. How her daughter could ever have fallen in love with such a despicable creature she would never know.

His mother-in-law's scorn piqued Wasp who was ever on the lookout for some way of getting his revenge on her. And so it was that one day he noticed that the twins, Atsu and Atsutse, were among the latest arrivals beneath the life-saving fruit tree. Now it was acknowledged throughout the land that the twins were far stronger than anyone else; nobody had ever successfully challenged their prowess, and so Wasp flew to Atsutse, saying,

"I would never dream of asking you for a favour in the normal run of events, Atsutse, but seeing that we live in extraordinary times, I do have a very great favour to ask you."

"Oh, yes. What's that then?"

"You may or not know that my mother-in-law has hated me from the day I married her daughter and so she never ceases to mock me, calling me spineless and feeble-bodied and she does it especially in front of my wife and children. I am wondering if you would be kind enough to engage in a fight with me right under my mother-in-law's nasty nose and to let me win the fight."

"Why should I risk my reputation for someone as evil as you?" asked Atsutse.

"If you do as I ask, I shall make sure that you and your brother, Atsu, receive the juiciest and most nutritious fruit from the life-giving tree," assured Wasp.

Trapped by the seriousness of the famine and drought, Atsutse agreed to the deal, knowing that should he and the others survive the current crisis, he would soon recover his dented reputation.

3

So the following day, Wasp engaged Atsutse in a fight which everyone was obliged to witness as they were all gathered in one place. A short way into the fight, Atsutse relaxed his muscles so that Wasp appeared to overpower him and was able to make a great show of roping him up and dragging him to the river, shouting triumphantly,

"So where's your great strength now, Atsutse?" Arriving at the river, Wasp did not untie Atsutse as they had previously agreed upon but said instead,

"I'm taking you far away, way down the river until we get to Chief Tsidi, an old friend of my father."

As soon as Atsutse realised that Wasp intended to abuse the favour that he had agreed to, he began to shout loudly for his twin brother, knowing that he at least would hear him and come immediately to his aid. Leaving his victim tied up on the river-bank, Wasp quickly flew to Atsu and filled his ears with wax to prevent him hearing his brother's call for help.

Returning to Atsutse, Wasp dragged him to Chief Tsidi's palace where he explained to the Chief that he was punishing this hard-hearted man who had persisted in eating the best fruit that fell from the life-giving tree when all around him were those who were dying for lack of food and drink. He, Wasp, was doing all he

Atsutse wrapped in a rope

could to help the starving people by dropping fruit onto the ground but his best endeavours were ruined by the all-consuming greed of this one evil man.

"Rope him tighter and carry him out to sea where you must leave him to drown!" ordered Chief Tsidi.

At this very moment, Hawk flew down to Atsu, pulled the wax out of his ears and told him what was happening to his brother. Whereupon, Atsu climbed onto the bird's back and the two flew with all speed until they reached the sea.

"Why are you drowning this man?" demanded Hawk.

Slow of thought, Wasp was unable to reply so while Hawk held the wretched insect captive, Atsu released Atsutse and used the rope to bind up Wasp.

Returning to Chief Tsidi's palace, they recounted the whole story. The Chief, angered by the way in which Wasp had betrayed his faith, provided even more ropes which they used to wrap round and round Wasp's waist until he could scarcely breathe. Not wanting to spend any more time with the snivelling Wasp, the twins dumped him on the ground as soon as they had left the village before continuing on their way back to the life-giving fruit tree where they had left all their family and friends.

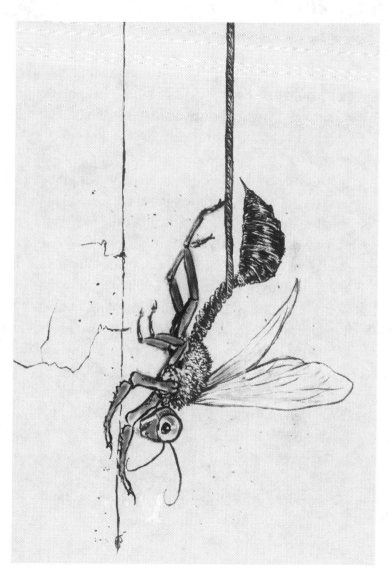

Wasp tighty roped up with a rope narrowing his waist

It did not take long for Wasp to decide that his skinny waist would bring forth nothing but howls of derisive laughter so he dragged himself to the nearest house with a thatched roof where he slowly crawled his way up the walls.

As soon as he reached the thatch, he buried himself in it so that no one could possibly see him.

In time the ropes disintegrated, but, disgraced and humiliated, Wasp decided that never again would he try and live with others. So it was and so it is that the wasp can always be found hiding in a thatch, ready to strike if you or I try and disturb him. And I advise you not to laugh at his pinched and puny waist. Not very manly is it? However, you laugh at your peril as Wasp does have a vicious sting in his tail.

> **Storyteller:** *This is the story an old lady told me on my way here to meet you.*
> **Audience:** *Is that so? Then long may your tongue be oiled.*
> **Storyteller:** *And long may your ears be greased.*
>
> **Storytelling village:** Have

Chapter 2

THE MAN, THE WOMAN AND
THE TWO CHILDREN

Storyteller: Listen to the story
Audience: So let the story begin
Storyteller: The story falls upon the Man
Audience: It falls upon the Man
Storyteller: The story falls upon the Woman
Audience: It falls upon the Woman
Storyteller: The story falls upon the Two Children
Audience: It falls upon the Two Children

Storyteller

Once upon a time, not here, not there, but somewhere, there was a village and in this village there lived a married couple, a Man and a Woman who, after several years, remained childless. The villagers talked about them, saying,

"So what is their problem? Is it him or her? What terrible sin has been committed in one of their families that they should not have children?"

Nobody knew but all had an opinion, so you can imagine the joy when the Woman fell pregnant, not once but twice. However, joy soon turned to pain when the second child was born and this too was a girl. Wanting sons, the Man threw the Two Children over the wall into the bush and left the house in anger.

The Woman quickly rescued the Two Children and nurtured them with great love and care while her husband was rarely seen at home as he put all his energies into running a prosperous farm. He was not much of a husband and even less of a father. Time went on until one day, the Man turned up at home and told his wife he needed his Two Children to protect his farm from birds and wild animals. About to refuse to allow him to take them, she suddenly agreed, telling him to return in a few days.

Calling her daughters to her, the Woman explained what their father wanted from them and taught them a song which they were to sing every time they were asked to scare the birds off the newly-sown seed.

Three days later the Man, their father, went to the farm and the Two Children left with him. Every time he instructed them to guard his seed, they sang the song the woman, their mother had taught them:

Father wanted a boy child, a boy child,
Mother delivered a girl child, a girl child.
Father threw us over the wall,
Father threw us over the wall.
If I had died, if we had died,
Who would work to scare the birds?
Who would work to scare the birds?
So Birds, fly down, so birds fly down.
Dig and swallow every grain.
Dig and swallow every grain.

Several days later, the Man visited the farm hoping to see the new shoots breaking through the freshly ploughed earth. Imagine his shock therefore, when not only was there not a shoot in sight but all his carefully sown seeds had vanished.

"So what is the meaning of this? What have you been doing, you idle girls?" shouted the Man.

The Two Children singing and dancing

"Do you really expect us to work for you and your wretched farm when you have done nothing for us from the day we were born? If we are only useless girls, why do you give us a job to do and then expect it to be done well?"

Their father had no good answer to this question and so he turned and disappeared for good, leaving the girls to run the farm with the Woman, their mother. They lived well on the prosperous, well-run farm but the Man had nothing but the hedgerows to sustain him and give him shelter for the rest of his days.

He had plenty of time to reflect upon the way in which he had treated his two children but did he ever think that he should have behaved differently? Well, maybe he did and maybe he didn't.

Storyteller: *An old lady told me this story on my way here to meet you*
Audience: *Is that so? Then long may your tongue be oiled*
Storyteller: *And long may your ears be greased*

Storytelling village: *Have*

The Woman and her two daughters working on the prosperous farm

Chapter 3

AYIYI, THE ANIMALS AND THE TERMITES

Storyteller: Listen to the story
Audience: So let the story begin
Storyteller: The story falls upon Ayiyi
Audience: It falls upon Ayiyi
Storyteller: The story falls upon the Animals
Audience: It falls upon the Animals
Storyteller: The story falls upon the Termites
Audience: It falls upon the Termites

Storyteller

Once upon a hungry time, there was no food for any of the villagers. Had the rains failed? Maybe. Had the crops been neglected? Maybe. Had the seeds been wasted? Maybe. Had the people offended their gods? Maybe. All we know for certain is that instead of the

15

usual hum and buzz of daily life, there was now scarcely a flicker as bodies and minds shut down, conserving every last drop of precious life.

Then who is it that, throughout all such times of devastation, is able to live where others die, to sing where others weep, to run where others stumble? Don't you know? Why, it's the Birds for whom the only problem is inconvenience as they have to rise a little earlier in the morning and return a little later in the evening, having completed a longer journey than usual. However, starvation does not threaten the Brids who always know where to find their daily food.

You will not be surprised to know that Ayiyi also found ways to survive during times of extreme hardship. His tricks were without number and so it happened this time that he begged the Birds to give him some feathers so that he too could fly to distant lands. The Birds would have refused him, but they knew better than to antagonise Ayiyi who would surely take his revenge in his own time. So Spider was given his feathers and the following morning he flew off with the Birds in eager anticipation of a special feast.

As they collected grain, Ayiyi declared to the Birds that the farm they were at belonged to his grandfather.

"This being the case, I forbid you to trespass on and plunder this farm again!" shouted Ayiyi.

"This being the case, you can give us back our feathers!" replied the Birds as they swooped down, removed their feathers and flew off, leaving Ayiyi stranded.

Could Ayiyi really be stranded? What do you think? He just laughed at the Birds and confidently set off walking. The first obstacle he came to was a river with a crocodile.

"Hey there, Croc! Want to earn a little cash instead of lazing around in the water?"

"What do you want me to do, Ayiyi? I know your games and on second thoughts I want nothing to do with you," replied Crocodile.

"No tricks, I promise. I'll never get across this river if I trick you, will I."

"Well, what do you want me to do?"

"Just give me a lift across the water. It'll be the easiest money you have ever earned."

"What will you give me then?" asked Crocodile, still hesitant.

"Well, it's like this. I haven't actually got any cash on me right now but I'll write an IOU on your back as you swim across and then everyone will see it. I can't deny something in my own handwriting, can I?"

Persuaded, Crocodile allowed Ayiyi to jump up on his back and, as they crossed the water, Ayiyi drew a silly face on Crocodile's back.

Ayiyi crossing the river on Crocodile's back

Reaching the other side, Crocodile asked Lizard to check what Ayiyi had written and so while Lizard was climbing up onto Crocodile's back, Ayiyi made his rapid get-away, disappearing into the forest in a trice.

So it was that an extremely angry Crocodile spent the next few weeks hunting for the despicable Spider until one day, thinking that he could see him in the distance, he struggled along the road under the fierce midday sun. Spotting Crocodile coming towards him, Ayiyi immediately began piling stones and boulders in a dip beside the road. Positioning himself beside an exceptionally large rock which lay a little distance from the dip, he pretended to push and pull, never once looking in Crocodile's direction.

"Ayiyi, at last I've caught up with you.

So you thought you could escape me but for once in your evil life you were wrong. Where's the money you owe me?"

Feigning surprise, Ayiyi replied,

"That's not a very friendly greeting, Crocodile. I'm sorry but I haven't the least idea of what you are talking about. What money? When? Why?"

"Aren't you that same Spider that I helped across the river? Isn't this your stupid idea of an IOU on my back? I suppose you know it won't come off either!"

Crocodile moving towards Ayiyi who is pretending to push a large rock

"I'm sorry, Crocodile, but you have got the wrong Ayiyi. As you can see, I'm in the quarrying business. It's years since I went near a river. Even the thought of water makes me feel panicky so I avoid it all costs. Still, no hard feelings in spite of your accusations. I tell you what, though. Just to show that we are friends, would you just pause a moment and help me lift this rock onto my head? As you can see, it's a particularly big one."

"Oh alright, but I'd rather practise with a smaller one first. I'm not used to this kind of thing."

So Crocodile attempted more or less successfully the first boulder and then agreed to help with the second, the really large, really heavy rock.

"Before we tackle this one, Croc, tell me which part of your body is the most vulnerable, the most sensitive? I don't want to hurt you."

"It's my head. So long as you avoid my head, I'll be fine."

Due to the rock's size and weight, Crocodile and Ayiyi agreed that they should both lift it but, just as it was poised above Crocodile's head, Ayiyi let go so the rock fell and smashed Crocodile's skull. Poor Crocodile's second defeat by Ayiyi was surely his final one.

Hiding the corpse among the boulders, Ayiyi went into the forest to find a gourd which he filled with foul-smelling poisonous gas. Returning to find Crocodile, he heaved him up onto his shoulders and set off on his next journey. After a while, he uncorked the gourd, allowing a little gas to escape to see if there was any living creature in the locality. Seeing a housefly collapse, Ayiyi realised that there must be humans living nearby so he continued on his way.

After two hours' travel, he came to a place where he was satisfied that he was well and truly on his own, so he put Crocodile on the ground and prepared a fire in order to cook him for his dinner. Just as he was about to eat, Lion, Leopard and Hyena appeared and as the aroma of the delicious dinner filled their nostrils, they finally succumbed to temptation and stole the crocodile soup the moment Ayiyi's back was turned.

What a mistake to make! Rare indeed is the creature who knowingly provokes Ayiyi. Realising in a trice what had happened, Ayiyi quickly planned his revenge and set off for his own village. He went straight to his house, found his children and immediately began reshaping their teeth so that all who saw them could not fail to be impressed by their beauty. Then he sent them to Lawokope where Lion, Leopard and Hyena

Lion, Leopard and Hyena stealing Ayiyi's pot of soup

lived, under the pretext of fetching live coals for their father's cooking pot.

"While you are in the village, make sure you smile and laugh with everyone you meet and when they ask, tell them that it was your father, the blacksmith, who styled your teeth so beautifully," instructed Ayiyi.

Travelling through Lawokope, the children saw Lion, Leopard and Hyena and, remembering their father's instructions, they showed their teeth off to their best advantage until the three Animals asked,

"Who made your teeth so beautiful?"

"Our father, the blacksmith. He is famous for his cosmetic surgery. Didn't you know?"

"Take us to him straightaway. I will not eat another meal with these misshapen teeth of mine!" commanded Lion.

"Nor me. I want every tooth in my head to be restored to its former glory," added Leopard.

After a few minutes, Hyena, always slow to voice his thoughts, said,

"I'm sure the food must taste far better if you have beautiful teeth."

"Well, given that you are all so keen to have the job done straightaway, you must follow us now and we will take you to our father," said Ayiyi's children. Without further ado, they all set off and Ayiyi, now well-disguised as a blacksmith, welcomed the three friends warmly, inviting them into his compound.

"You must realise, my friends, that what you want me to do is very painful although I can guarantee that it is well worth all the suffering in the long run. As I need you to be absolutely still while I operate, I must stretch you between two trees and then tie your limbs to the trees so that, however severe the pain, you will not move a muscle. Without this preliminary procedure, the operation will fail."

Nervous but determined, the three Animals agreed and Ayiyi stretched and tied their limbs very securely between four conveniently placed trees before asking his children to fetch the fresh crocodile stew he had made. Placing it on the ground in front of them, Ayiyi started eating, savouring every mouthful and tossing the bones high in the air in the direction of the three starving, suffering Animals. Try as they might, they could not catch the bones which flew tantalisingly past them. Their mission completed, Ayiyi and his children left the village.

Three days later, a column of Termites happened to pass by and the three Animals, their voices faint and weak, nevertheless managed to attract the attention of the

Termites, pleading with them to eat the sticks which Ayiyi had used to lash them to the trees.

"Certainly not", said their leader. "Many is the time we have done someone a good deed and what do we ever get back? How will we be rewarded?"

"Just state your terms and we will do all in our power to meet your demands," replied Lion and Leopard together.

"I have money put aside for an important occasion and nothing can be more important than saving my life," added Hyena.

So, encouraged by the promises, the Termites gave in, destroyed the wooden ties and helped the three weak Animals find their feet and their way home. Exhausted but elated, the three friends set a date for the Termites to come and feast with them, by way of thanks. The Termites were delighted and spent many a happy hour imagining all the good things they would eat and drink.

Ayiyi, whose eyes and ears picked up on everything, got to hear of the forthcoming feast. Just a few hours before the appointed time, he sent an anonymous message to the Termites, postponing the party until a later date, explaining that Lion had unexpectedly fallen ill and needed a few days to recover his health. The master trickster then prepared himself and his children for the feast, applying red clay to their mouths so that, for all the world, one would think that they were termites. Satisfied with their disguise, they set off for Lawokope, singing as they marched:

We are the children of the Termite mounds,
Termite mounds, Termite mounds.
And we freed the captive Animals,
Animals, Animals.
We come in glory to share the feast,
Share the feast, share the feast.
Let the Animals give us food,
Let the Animals give us drink,
Give us food, give us drink.
Let the earth be silent now,
Let us hear the ancient sound,
Hunu baye loo, hunu baye loo.

Completely duped, the Animals received Ayiyi and his children as friends, showering them with gifts and waiting on them with a delicious assortment of food and drink. As the big red sun sank in the sky announcing the close of day, Ayiyi took his leave of the Animals and he and his children went on their merry way home.

Now let us return to the Termites and we find them a few weeks later, setting out for Lawokope on the rearranged day for the feast. As they went they also sang a song which was so similar to the one sung by Ayiyi and his children that the Animals were convinced that they were about to receive a most unwanted visit from the villainous Ayiyi, up to one of his tricks again. Deciding there and then to punish him for his impudent behaviour, they hastily put water on to boil and then sat and waited. When the visitors arrived they greeted them warmly and showed them to a room saying,

"You may wish to rest a while in here after your long and tiring journey. If you will excuse us, we will just put the finishing touches to the meal. We want everything to be perfect."

With these words, the Animals fetched the boiling water and, returning to the room, poured it over the hapless Termites, killing all but one. The lone survivor realised that some treachery was afoot and decided to investigate.

"Did you or did you not send word to us that Lion was ill so that you were obliged to change the day of the feast?"

"Certainly not. We had our feast on the day we had arranged. But you were there so what on earth are you talking about?"

Question led to question and it was not long before Lion, Leopard, Hyena and the Termite realised that, once again, they had all suffered at Ayiyi's treacherous hands. How could the Animals find words to express their sorrow and regret for killing the termites? All any of them could do was track down and kill Ayiyi. They had to rid the community of this fiend who clearly had no conscience at all. But how? How could they get rid of the devilish Spider who had always outwitted those who stood between him and his desires?

A few days later, Ayiyi was seen walking boldly through Lawokope and the Animals rushed out and gave chase. Ayiyi ran for dear life, slipping into a convenient hole in the ground at the very moment the Animals were about to seize hold of him. Now this hole happened to be the entrance to the home of a family of land crabs who, naturally enough, were surprised at this sudden intrusion into their privacy.

"Just what do you think you are doing, Ayiyi? Is this another of your evil tricks?" asked Crab.

It was while Spider was spinning a tale to the Crabs, that our old friends Lion, Leopard and Hyena called Pig over and asked him to use his long nose to excavate the hole and capture Ayiyi. Always willing to help in a

Pig sniffing around a hole

plan to capture the wicked Spider, Pig began digging around the hole.

However, with his sharp ears, Ayiyi had overheard the conversation with Pig and so, thinking very quickly, he apologised for the abruptness of his arrival in their home and told the Crabs that he was excited as he had managed to find them some delicious meat, which was about to be delivered to their hole.

"I have had the good fortune to be offered a large quantity of meat, which I would like to share with you, my friends. It will be here at any moment now, so sharpen your knives and enjoy the feast!" ordered Ayiyi.

No sooner had they done this than Pig's long nose appeared, pushing through the tunnel leading into the Crabs' home. CHOP! went the first knife, slicing through the tempting snout and CHOP! CHOP! CHOP! went the second, third and fourth knives. Poor Pig was squealing and kicking but unable to retreat as Lion, Leopard and Hyena were intent on pushing him down into the hole just as far as they could, so determined were they to catch Ayiyi.

Lion, Leopard and Hyena pushing Pig

Pig's snout became shorter and shorter and shorter until finally it protruded no further than his mouth.

And so it was and so it is from that day to this that the Pig is known all over the world not for his kindness and cooperation with Lion, Leopard and Hyena but for his short, flat, ugly snout. As for Ayiyi, was he caught or did he escape? Well, what do you think?

> *Storyteller: An old lady told me this story on my way here to meet you*
> *Audience: Is that so? Then long may your tongue be oiled*
> *Storyteller: And long may your ears be greased*

Storytelling village: *Anyako*

Chapter 4

AYIYI, THE CHIEF AND THE CHILLIES

Storyteller: Listen to the story
Audience: So let the story begin
Storyteller: The story falls upon Ayiyi
Audience: It falls upon Ayiyi
Storyteller: The story falls upon the Chief
Audience: It falls upon the Chief

Storyteller

Once upon a time it so happened that there lived a Chief who had a very beautiful daughter. Whilst he wanted his daughter to marry, he wanted only the very best of all the men both far and wide to be his son-in-law and so he decided to set a test which would surely eliminate all those who fell short of the ideal person he so desired.

Accordingly, he sent for a very large quantity of chilli peppers which he ordered to be ground into a paste. When his large earthenware bowl was full, he commanded that the gong-gong should be beaten to summon all the villagers from all around to the palace compound. In they trooped, the short and the tall, the thin and the fat, the handsome and the ugly, the rich and the poor, the intelligent and the stupid, the young and the old.

"Any man wishing to claim the hand of my beautiful daughter in marriage must first prove his worth. He must eat this bowl of chilli paste under the close scrutiny of my Elders. Should any man pause or flinch whilst eating, he will be disqualified immediately."

Undeterred by the enormity of the task, the suitors lined up to try and win the hand of the Chief's daughter. After a long line of failures it seemed that the challenge was truly an impossible one. Would the Chief ever find anyone who could succeed at such a task? It seemed not, and the air was thick and menacing with failure and despondency when all of a sudden they heard,

"Let there be silence!"

Stepping forward, bold as ever, Ayiyi went on to ask the Chief,

"Is it true that you don't know how to make a sucking or a hissing sound?"

"Yes, that is true," answered the Chief, bemused by Ayiyi's sudden appearance in his royal compound.

"Would you like to be able to make the sounds that everyone else can make?"

"Of course I would. A chief should be able to do everything."

"Will you allow a competitor to sing while he attempts to eat the chilli paste?"

"I can see no objection to that," replied the Chief, still bemused.

So Ayiyi took the bowl of chilli paste and started singing:

"We all say 'sssss', yes, we all say 'sssss'.
Big men say 'sssss' and small men say 'sssss'.
The rich man says 'sssss' and the poor man says 'sssss'.
Young men say 'sssss' and old men say 'sssss'.
My brother says 'sssss' and my sister says 'sssss'.
The Lion says 'sssss' and the Monkey says 'sssss'.

Ayiyi before the Chief and the Princess

The Chief says 'sssss' and Ayiyi says 'sssss'.
We all say 'sssss', yes, we all say 'sssss'.

As he sang, inhaling and then exhaling deeply with every 'sssss', Ayiyi ate every last mouthful of chilli paste so you may well imagine the consternation and fury his success caused amongst the assembled villagers.

"How is it that that wretched, that despicable Ayiyi has managed to eat all that chilli paste? How is it that he can be allowed to marry the Chief's daughter? Is it not enough that we already have to live with all his tricks, his lies, his deceptions?"

The Chief, equally disturbed by the prospect of having Ayiyi as his son-in-law, but forced to honour his pledge, was quick to cut them short.

"Whatever you may feel, my people, it cannot be denied that Ayiyi has won my daughter's hand in marriage. Now be off with you all!"

So the villagers made their way home, dispirited and disgruntled while the Chief held a banquet in the palace to which he invited his Queen Mother and his Elders. Ayiyi, delirious with self-congratulation as he reflected on his achievement in receiving the Chief's daughter as his bride, ate and drank to excess.

Ayiyi stuffing himself with food and drink

This was by no means the first time that Ayiyi had indulged his appetite but never before had so much depended on his proper behaviour. Alas, during his wedding night, Ayiyi was seized by the most excruciating stomach cramps. They could mean only one thing, but where was the toilet? There was no toilet nearby; there was no toilet anywhere around.

Unable to restrain himself, Ayiyi's stomach took over and the bedroom became his toilet. The Chief's daughter fled in horror and Ayiyi, ashamed for the first time in his life, scuttled to a corner of the room and up the wall to the eaves. Here he found a small hole through which he escaped and, finding himself on the outside of the building he ran as fast as his eight wobbly legs would carry him. He only stopped when he came to the forest where he could hide himself away, away from the Chief, away from the Chief's beautiful daughter and away from the mockery of the villagers.

And so it was and so it is from that day to this that, unlike the housefly who is always there to annoy, Spider keeps himself to himself, desperately hoping that you will never see him.

Ayiyi running away from the village

Storyteller: *An old lady told me this story on my way here to meet you*

Audience: *Is that so? Then long may your tongue be oiled*

Storyteller: *And long may your ears be greased*

Storytelling village: *Anyako*

Chapter 5

THE GOAT FARMER AND THE THIEF

Storyteller: Listen to my story
Audience: So let the story begin
Storyteller: The story falls upon the Goat Farmer
Audience: It falls upon the Goat Farmer
Storyteller: The story falls upon the Thief
Audience: It falls upon the Thief

Storyteller

Once upon a time, as I have been told, there lived a prosperous Farmer in a remote village. Being wealthy, he had built himself a beautiful house surrounded by a wall so high that, try as they might, envious eyes were unable to pry.

Now this Farmer had many goats which he kept in the house where they roamed freely during the day. Every night, however, the goats were rounded up, put into a pen in the house and the gate was secured firmly by the Farmer himself. Happy in the knowledge that he, his family and his goats were safe, the Farmer went to bed where he fell into a deep sleep. Neither the Farmer nor his wife and children were ever known to wake at night.

So it was with great astonishment that one morning the Farmer realised that some of his goats were missing. He questioned his wife. He questioned his children. He searched the house from top to bottom. He searched all round the compound. But not a single lost goat was to be found. Dismayed, the Farmer toured the village and then set off for a neighbouring village. His efforts were all to no avail.

On his way home, he met a blacksmith to whom he recounted his strange and worrying story.

"I just don't understand it," lamented the poor Farmer.

"If you want my advice, what you need is an iron trap," replied the blacksmith, seizing the opportunity to make a sale.

"Very well. Have it ready for me tomorrow!" said the Farmer as he handed over the money.

So the following morning, the Farmer arrived to collect the trap which the blacksmith showed him how to set. That evening he followed all the instructions and then went to his bedroom, carrying the iron chain which was attached to the trap. Before climbing into bed, he secured the other end of this same chain to his bed and then settled down to sleep.

During the night, the goat thieves arrived. Scaling the high wall round the compound, the thieves quickly broke into the Farmer's house ready to steal more goats. As they climbed into the goat pen, their leader trod on the iron trap and, in an instant, he was held tight, unable to move. All attempts to free his leg failed and so, in desperation, the thieves decided that they would have to carry away their leader with the trap still attached to him. As they began to move him, the chain tightened and the Farmer's bed started to jerk across the floor. In an instant, the Farmer awoke, seized his gun and fired into the air.

Frightened out of their wits, the thieves fled, leaving their leader to his fate. Not knowing what was going to happen to him, the Thief sang quietly:

Agbodzaku[1] has consumed our very roots.
Mother Awaworli[2] has destroyed us.
The aged are no longer amongst us.
Salagatsi[3] has taken us all.
Mother Death has total dominion.
Agbodzaku has consumed our very roots.
Mother Awaworli has destroyed us.

Presuming that all the thieves must have run away upon hearing the gun shots, the Farmer stayed in bed until dawn. Imagine his surprise when he came downstairs and found the leader of the thieves caught in the trap. After raising the alarm, the Farmer took the man, still attached to the trap, to the village Chief who summoned all his Elders to preside over the case. The trap having been removed, the Chief began to interrogate the Thief.

"So what made you steal from the Goat Farmer?" asked the Chief.

"The Farmer is already rich and I am only a poor man. To have a few goats to sell is the beginning of my way out of poverty," explained the Thief.

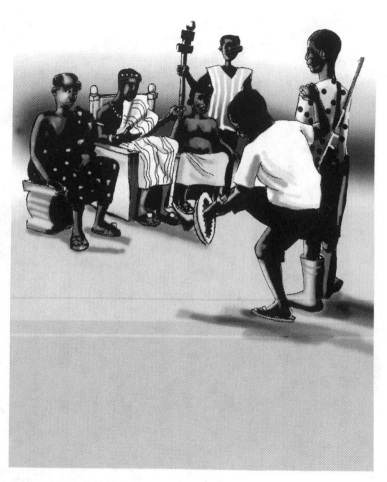

The Thief with the iron trap and the Farmer before the Chief

"So you admit to having already stolen from the Farmer?"

"Yes, I do," replied the Thief.

"And you admit intending to steal again last night?" asked one of the Elders.

"Yes, of course."

"We sentence you to a public flogging so that you may serve as an example to the whole community. We will not tolerate thieves taking advantage of defenseless people," declared the Chief.

Upon hearing this, the Thief started to laugh.

"Why are you laughing?" asked the astonished Chief. Still laughing, the Thief asked permission to sing a song.

"Very well," replied the Chief.

So the Chief and his Elders listened as the Thief faced them and sang:

Farmer, Goat Farmer,
Listen to me! Listen to me!
Why sleep and sleep?
Why sleep and sleep?
You sleep too much,
You sleep too much.
With a thud, with a bang, with a crash,

I jumped over your wall,
I jumped over your wall.
Farmer, Goat Farmer,
Listen to me! Listen to me!
Why sleep and sleep?
Why sleep and sleep?
You sleep too much,
You sleep too much.

Impressed with such a frank confession, the court considered the Thief's case carefully before reaching their final verdict. At last the Chief stood, paused for a few moments and then, speaking through his linguist[4], he addressed the Thief, saying, "This court has looked at the facts of your case and, having taken into account both your actual theft of goats, your intended theft of more goats and also your behaviour here before us, we have decided on the following course of action. You will receive an official caution endorsed by this court, followed by an official pardon similarly endorsed by this court. Your Chief and Elders insist that you learn a trade or enter into a profession which will enable you to earn money so that you will no longer need to steal from others."

"Thank you all very much. I am indeed indebted to you for your kindness. I shall do as you request," replied the Thief, no longer laughing.

True to his word, the Thief found an apprenticeship with a blacksmith and began to make the farm implements which were in constant demand. Everyone needed at least a hoe and a scythe and so, over time he became not only an accomplished blacksmith but also a well-respected member of the community. He never forgot what had happened to him in his earlier days and whenever he was working in his forge he could be heard singing:

Farmer, Goat Farmer,
Listen to me! Listen to me!
Why sleep and sleep?
Why sleep and sleep?
You sleep too much,
You sleep too much.
With a thud, with a bang, with a crash,
I jumped over your wall,
I jumped over your wall.
Farmer, Goat Farmer,
Listen to me! Listen to me!
Why sleep and sleep?
Why sleep and sleep?
You sleep too much,
You sleep too much.

The Thief at his workshop

So, my friends, you can see that the man who mends his ways and learns a trade or enters into a profession is indeed fortunate. He is a man with a future.

Storyteller: *This is the story an old lady told me on my way here to meet you*
Audience: *Is that so? Then long may your tongue be oiled*
Storyteller: *And long may your ears be greased*

Storytelling village: *Klikor*

Notes
[1], [2] and [3] - *Agbodzaku* , *Awaworli* and *Salagatsi* are all personifications of death.
[4] *'Linguist'* - the man whose role it is to speak the words which are used in a conversation between the chief and those who are granted an audience with him.
There is no direct conversation between the chief and those who communicate with him in his official capacity.

Chapter 6

THE FATHER AND THE
THREE SONS

Storyteller: Listen to the story
Audience: So let the story begin
Storyteller: The story falls upon the Father
Audience: It falls upon the Father
Storyteller: The story falls upon the Three Sons
Audience: It falls upon the Three Sons

Storyteller

Long, long ago, when our ancestors took no account
of the passage of time, there lived a young man who
decided he should at last marry. It was not long before
he met a beautiful girl and her parents happily gave

their consent to the marriage. All the necessary rites were performed and so it was that the two began their life together.

The man, Mekam, was a hard-working farmer but his wife, Sedina, was particularly lazy, barely doing the minimum that was required to look after their Three Sons, let alone her husband and the house.

"Look at this house! Dust and dirt everywhere! All the clothes need either washing or ironing. Food has to be bought and then cooked. Am I supposed to spend my whole life in drudgery? What's the point of cleaning? The minute I turn my back everything is dirty again!"

Listening to this tirade day after day, Mekam became increasingly despondent and decided that the only way forward was to seek a divorce from Sedina. Accordingly, he returned to her parents, taking her with him and complaining to them that their daughter was an unworthy wife, doing little or nothing at home. Moreover, she took no responsibility for the behaviour of their first-born Son who barely spoke and did nothing either for himself or for those around him. Mekam's parents-in-law listened to him and then his father-in-law said, "Are you saying that a woman who has borne you Three Sons has brought nothing to your marriage? She has given you the greatest gift of all. Through your children your life will go on, way into the future. Go home and take our daughter with you. Show proper care for your wife and for your Three Sons and then they will show you love and respect in their turn."

So Mekam and Sedina returned home and life continued in much the same way until it happened one day that the man went into the forest taking his three sons with him. Suddenly, Mekam heard a distant growling and quickly realised that a lion was fast approaching. Never in his life having been faced with such danger, Mekam turned to his children, saying, "What shall we do? Where shall we hide? The lion is far faster and more powerful than us. Is there any way we can save our lives?"

His two favourite Sons, the second and last-born said together, "We will lie here in wait and as soon as the lion appears we will stone it until we kill it."

They were all amazed when the first-born Son suddenly spoke clearly, "We should climb a tree and wait until the lion passes on his way beneath us."

"Senseless boy! Why do you speak now, only to make stupid suggestions? Do you not understand the danger we are in?"

As ever, Mekam was quick to condemn his oldest Son. Drawing away from his father and nearer his brothers, the boy repeated, "We should climb a tree and wait until the lion passes on his way beneath us."

To Mekam's astonishment, the two younger Sons agreed and followed their brother up into a tall tree. Their father, however, started collecting stones which he piled beside him and sat down to wait, confident that he would overpower the mighty beast. It was not long before the lion appeared and moved towards the farmer who quickly grabbed his stones. Before he could even throw the first one, the wild animal leaped towards him, roaring and shaking his majestic mane. Moments later, Mekam lay dead and the lion hoisted him on his shoulder to carry him back to his lair and enjoy a hearty feast.

Once they were certain that all danger had passed, the Three Sons came down from the tree and returned home where their mother greeted them with open arms.

The Lion leaping towards the Father

"Where have you been? What have you been doing? Where is your father?"

Recounting their story first to their mother and then to neighbours, it was agreed by all that Mekam had received just punishment for the way in which he had always treated his first-born Son. A good and wise parent must know that every son and daughter must be shown equal affection and respect. After all, which of us knows when one of our children may one day hold the key to our own life?

> *Storyteller:* An old woman told me this story on my way here to meet you.
>
> *Audience:* Is that so? Then long may your tongue be oiled.
>
> *Storyteller:* And long may your ears be greased.
>
> *Storytelling village:* Have

Chapter 7

THE PRINCESS AND THE DOG

Storyteller: Listen to the story
Audience: So let the story begin
Storyteller: The story falls upon the Princess
Audience: It falls upon the Princess
Storyteller: The story falls upon the Dog
Audience: It falls upon the Dog

Storyteller

I have never met them and you have certainly never met them but once upon a time there was a celebrated royal family, known throughout the land and beyond. Why were they well known? Well, it was all because of the great beauty of their one and only child, the Royal Princess. Her flawless complexion, her sparkling eyes, her silken hair, her melodious voice and her perfectly proportioned body were the stuff of dreams and yet she was real. Or was she? Certainly her parents believed she was and so too did the many suitors who came seeking her hand in marriage. For they came young and old, tall and short, fat and thin, rich and poor, intelligent and not so intelligent.

In our eagerness to praise her beauty, we have forgotten her foremost attribute; her willingness to do everything her parents wished her to do without a murmur of protest. The day dawned, however, when our flawless heroine refused to cooperate with her parents. What was the issue? It was indeed the choice of a husband. Why, she asked herself, should her parents choose the man to whom she was to be attached for the rest of her life? She simply would not allow them to do so and in the end, after many anguished hours, the King and Queen relented and waited to see just who their daughter would select for her marriage partner. Would it be a prince from a rival kingdom? Would it be a prince from an impoverished family? Would it be a prince from a far distant land who would take her away so that they would never see their precious daughter again?

Implausible as it may seem, this beautiful girl chose the Dog; yes indeed, the very Dog who had come begging her to marry him. At this, not only her parents but the whole land was thrown into disbelief, consternation and fury.

The Princess dancing with the Dog

How could she insult them like this? How could they possibly continue to show support and loyalty? How could anyone respect, let alone love Dog who spent his life scavenging, eating whatever he sniffed out in every refuse dump in the kingdom? Were they now to endure him sniffing round the royal banquet table?

The Princess, however, was deaf to all pleading and shut herself away, refusing all food and drink. Thus it was that the King and Queen, fearing for their daughter's life, consented to the union and even gave her and Dog the glorious ceremony which her royal position demanded. The Princess and Dog were resplendent in their gorgeous marriage robes. We cannot go so far as to say that there was great rejoicing throughout the land but the appointed day arrived and people being what people are, they enjoyed the feasting and dancing which went on for a whole week.

What nobody knew was that the Princess found Dog's scavenging habits as unpleasant as everyone else and she had only consented to marry Dog on condition that he mended his ways and ate in a way that befitted his new station in life. For a while, Dog did exactly as he was told and there was nothing but happiness in the

The Princess dancing with The Dog

household but, little by little, people began whispering that they had seen him sniffing around his old haunts.

"Is it true that you have been searching for food in all the places I have forbidden you to go?" asked the Princess.

Dog could not deny it as he knew that there had been too many sightings for him to even think of concealing the truth.

"But why does it matter? It doesn't mean that I love you any the less," replied Dog.

The atmosphere in the house became more and more strained as the Princess realised that she was powerless to stop her husband resuming his old ways. Unable to bear the disgrace and humiliation any longer, the Princess took her own life. The once-happy couple had one friend and one friend only and so it was he, Black Ant who tried to comfort Dog in his grief and who agreed to accompany him as he went to break the dreadful news to the King and Queen. As they journeyed they sang a song which they hoped would be heard as they approached the palace:

This was our way of life,
This is the way life was.

She never smiled,
So I never smiled.
This was our way of life.
One day I smiled at my wife,
But she didn't smile at me.
My wife ran away,
So I ran away.
This is what happened one day.
She left and killed herself,
She killed herself that day.
She never smiled,
So I never smiled.
This was our way of life.

As Dog and Black Ant arrived at the palace, the King and Queen were standing at the entrance, listening to the chant which brought them the unexpected and terrible news.

"Go back to your miserable house and bury the body of the Princess. We can never bury her here, such is the disgrace she has brought upon us and upon her ancestors. Leave this palace and never show yourself or your miserable friend to us again!" commanded the King.

Black Ant and Dog approaching the King and Queen

So the two returned, dug a deep hole in the forest and half-carried, half-dragged the body of the Princess to the forest. On their way, there was a heavy downpour which drenched Dog, Black Ant and the body which I hesitate to tell you was already in an advanced state of decomposition.

By the time they had buried the Princess, Ant's body was covered in human matter and so it was and so it is from that day to this that Black Ant is condemned to carry the stench of death wherever he goes. Until his own death, Dog was seen sniffing and eating at every dump in the neighbourhood, and fathers throughout the kingdom reminded their daughters of the fate which befell the obstinate Princess. Did they take heed? I don't know. Do you?

Storyteller: *An old lady told me this story on my way here to meet you*
Audience; *Is that so? Then long may your tongue be oiled*
Storyteller: *And long may your ears be greased*

Storytelling village: *Have*

Chapter 8

THE FROG AND THE LIZARD

Storyteller: Listen to the story
Audience: So let the story begin
Storyteller: The story falls upon the Frog
Audience: It falls upon the Frog
Storyteller: The story falls upon the Lizard
Audience: It falls upon the Lizard

Storyteller

Once upon a happy time before animals learned to be fearful of man, Lizard invited Frog for a swim.

"We could even have a race," he added, hopefully.

"You are joking, aren't you?" replied Frog.

"I suppose you think I've forgotten how to swim just because I'm usually sunning myself on a plant or a rock."

"Not at all," said Lizard, feeling rather snubbed.

"I thought it would be a friendly and pleasant way to while away a few hours on this hot, lazy afternoon."

"I tell you what, my old friend, let's just accept that I am bound to be a much better swimmer than you are and then I can go back to my afternoon snooze."

"If you think you're so good, you should set about proving it instead of making idle claims," challenged Lizard.

"Okay, if you're so determined, that's exactly what I shall do. Come on, we'll go to Alligator's house and use him as our referee."

Having arrived at Alligator's house, Frog explained the situation to him. Alligator listened carefully and, turning to face them both, he said,

"I have my doubts about your superior swimming skills, Lizard, but to spur you on I will give you half my kingdom if you manage to beat Frog. After all, I do enjoy a good contest. You must both be here and ready to compete seven days from now, at nine in the morning."

So it happened that seven days later, Lizard arrived at the river, but there was no sign of Frog.

"Well, that just says it all. He's all mouth, that Frog. He knew he would lose, didn't he. What a coward he is," complained Lizard to Alligator.

"I'm not so sure you're right, Lizard. Let's just wait a bit," replied Alligator, worried about what would happen to the half kingdom he had offered if Frog really did fail to turn up. Would Lizard argue that he had beaten Frog, fair and square?

When some half an hour later, Frog came leaping along the river path, he apologised profusely, explaining, "You see, few people know that I have full responsibility for the day-to-day care of my children. My wife leaves for work early in the morning and doesn't return until mid-evening. She has a very important job, you know."

"So what exactly was more pressing than getting here on time?" asked Lizard aggressively.

"Oh, just the usual chores. You know, preparing breakfast, getting the children off to school, hanging the washing out, cleaning the house, sweeping the yard and doing a bit of shopping."

Having no good answer, Lizard just glared and said.

"Well, let's start the contest before you think of something else you need to do!"

Frog and Lizard marched to the river where they lined up side by side and waited for Alligator to give the order to jump in.

"On your marks, get set, go!"

For a few strokes, they were neck and neck but it wasn't long before Frog took the lead and landed on

The Frog and the Lizard ready to jump into the river

the opposite bank. Looking back, he saw Lizard who was only about halfway across.

After a few moments, Frog began taunting Lizard as he shouted with all his might.

"Come on, Lizard. Make an effort! Start swimming, not paddling! I'm waiting for you."

Everyone who happened to be passing by stopped to see what was going on, and it wasn't long before a great crowd started chanting, "Go, Lizard, go! Go! Go! Go! Swim, Lizard, swim! Swim! Swim! Swim!"

Poor old Lizard was making no progress at all. In fact, it was all he could do to splutter a few words.

"I'm puffed out! Help, Frog! Help! I'm puffed out! Help, Frog! Help!"

All the spectators burst out laughing but as Lizard started to vanish under the water and then bob up again, gulping and gasping, Alligator realised that he was indeed in difficulty.

"Go and help him, Frog!"

"Certainly not. He wanted this contest and now he's got it!"

"But you don't want to see the silly creature die, do you?" entreated Alligator.

"Oh, very well. He'd better be grateful and stop all this silly nonsense. Everyone knows that a frog can swim better than a lizard."

So Frog leaped back into the water and, with two strokes of his muscular legs, he was at Lizard's side, saying, "Hop up on my back and I'll take you to the bank."

Frog carrying Lizard to the river bank

A few moments later, Lizard collapsed upon dry land, gasping and panting. Frog jumped up on his back, pumping hard with his front feet until Lizard choked up all the water he had swallowed. Seeing that Lizard was not in fact going to die, Frog went to join Alligator and the two of them shared a good chuckle. Lizard, however, was definitely not in a chuckling mood and so as soon as he could move again, he ran off into the forest where he climbed a tree, out of sight of all those who were longing to catch a glimpse of him and enjoy a bit of mockery.

And so it was and so it is to this day that whenever you see Lizard, he is either scuttling past, running up a wall or a tree, or he is doing his press-ups in the hope that one day he will indeed be strong enough to beat Frog.

Storyteller: This is the story an old woman told me on my way here to meet you
Audience: Is that so? Then long may your tongue be oiled
Storyteller: And long may your ears be greased

Storytelling village: *Dzelukope*

Chapter 9

THE CATFISH AND THE BIRDS

Storyteller: Listen to the story
Audience: So let the story begin
Storyteller: The story falls upon on the Catfish
Audience: It falls upon the Catfish
Storyteller: The story falls upon the Birds
Audience: It falls upon the Birds

Storyteller

Once upon a time there was great hunger not here, not there, but somewhere in the land where the Catfish and the Birds lived. As the rains had failed, the crops had withered and cattle lay dead and dying on the land they usually grazed. Desolation was all around.

The Catfish and The Birds

There was, however, one exception in this world where each day was a struggle for survival. The Birds were able to fly great distances and so every evening they could be seen returning to their favourite tree with all the food they had found that day. Now this tree overhung a pond which was home to the Catfish who was having great problems finding enough to eat. Imagine therefore Catfish's outrage when he had first to witness the Birds returning with their feast, and then to endure their droppings in his pond, since they sat and ate on the same bare branches of the same tree overhanging the same pond evening after evening. So, late one evening, Catfish approached the leader of the Birds, saying,

"Excuse me, Bird, where do you go to find your food?"

"Go? Go? Where do we go? Oh, it's far too hard to explain," replied the leader.

"Well, can I come with you? Please!" wheedled Catfish.

"What? What? Come with us? You? Oh, I suppose so, but you must be ready to leave at four, no, three in the morning," replied Bird, somewhat grudgingly.

"'That's not a problem but how shall I travel with you? You know I haven't any wings."

"This certainly calls for a serious meeting with my family. Stay here and I should be back later."

Catfish waited and waited. After what seemed a very long time, Bird returned and explained that it had been agreed that each bird should contribute a few feathers for Catfish to attach to his body and use as wings.

Had you been looking up at the sky at dawn the following morning, you would have seen a flock of Birds and a Catfish flying eastwards towards the sun.

After two hours they reached Ajayi's farm where the Birds immediately swooped onto the crops and started collecting food for the day. Catfish, unable to control his greed after weeks of near starvation, became very quarrelsome and tried to lay claim to all the crops.

"I have already chosen that millet," asserted Catfish.

"But you are taking your fill of the maize," retorted the Birds.

"I need millet as well. I haven't eaten for weeks."

It wasn't long before the Birds decided to leave Catfish and go in search of another farm. Such ingratitude from Catfish was not to be tolerated.

"We've had enough of your attitude. Give us back our feathers!" demanded the Birds.

"Not likely," came Catfish's aggressive and cocky response.

Catfish with the Birds flying towards a crop farm

Undeterred, the Birds descended on Catfish, removed the feathers and flew off together just before Ajayi, the farmer, appeared to investigate the commotion which had roused him from his sleep. Finding Catfish among his crops, Ajayi became very angry and determined to catch and punish this intruder.

"How dare you take my crops, you thieving, good-for-nothing catfish!" bellowed the farmer. Fear paralysed Catfish who found himself cornered.

"Please stop, Ajayi, Mr. Farmer, Sir. You're making a big mistake. It's the birds who brought me here today and it's the Birds who have been coming every day, stripping your crops bare."

"What birds?" roared the farmer.

"They have just flown off, Ajayi, leaving me here all alone. How do you expect me to escape?"

"Same way as you got here, I suppose."

"Well I can't, not now. But let's not talk about all that. I know you are angry, Ajayi, and I do understand why, but before you kill me let me sing you a song. It's the very least I can do after I have caused you so much distress," pleaded Catfish in whose wily mind a plan was just emerging.

Now let it be understood that Catfish was renowned for his beautiful singing voice and so Ajayi, who enjoyed a good tune, agreed to the suggestion.

"This performance of yours had better be good, in fact more than good. I'm in no mood to play games with you."

Screwing up his courage, Catfish immediately began to sing for his life:

Ajayi, I did not know your farm was here,
It was the dove who brought me here.
Ajayi, I did not know your farm was here,
It was the pigeon who brought me here.
Ajayi, I did not know your farm was here,
It was the hawk who brought me here.
Ajayi, I did not know your farm was here,
It was the raven who brought me here.
Ajayi, I did not know your farm was here,
It was the birds who brought me here.

While Catfish was singing, the farmer started tapping his feet in time with the song and very soon he was dancing. He danced up one field and down another, round his house and round his garden, over and over again. Such was his enjoyment that he forgot all about the thieving Catfish who bit by bit, little by little, slid and slithered his way across the fields until he reached the farmer's pond where it was the matter of an instant to dive to the muddy bottom, out of sight.

The Farmer dancing to the Catfish's song

Thus it was that Catfish, who you may know as the Mudfish, escaped Ajayi, but from that day forth he has been condemned to living in the water and feeding on whatever he can find around him. As for the Birds and Ajayi, life continued in the way that it had always done. Some years were years of plenty and some were lean, some were happy and some were not.

Storyteller: *This is the story an old lady told me on my way here to meet you.*
Audience: *Is that so? Then long may your tongue be oiled.*
Storyteller: *And long may your ears be greased.*

Storytelling village: *Klikor*

Chapter 10

THE RACOON, THE RAT
AND THE LEOPARD

Storyteller: Listen to the story
Audience: So let the story begin
Storyteller: The story falls upon the Racoon
Audience: It falls upon the Racoon
Storyteller: The story falls upon the Rat
Audience: It falls upon the Rat
Storyteller: The story falls upon the Leopard
Audience: It falls upon the Leopard

Storyteller

Once upon a very long time ago, there lived a Racoon and a Rat who had been friends for as long as either of them could remember. Rarely was one to be seen without the other. There were many reasons for their friendship but, in order to understand this story, my friends, you need to remember that they both loved mutton. In fact, they loved every cut of the meat and every dish that came from a sheep or a lamb; lamb chops, stewing lamb, shoulder of lamb, leg of lamb, mutton stew, minced lamb, lamb kebab and all the others that you can think of.

You will not be surprised, therefore, to learn that Racoon and Rat were regularly tempted to steal a sheep from the flock. Such was their passion for the meat that the flock began to dwindle at an alarming rate and so, one day, the shepherd sent for Leopard.

"Leopard, instead of your usual roaming, I want you to stay with my sheep and protect them from danger, particularly at night."

"What's in it for me?" asked Leopard, as he was particularly fond of his night-time wandering.

"There will be a big reward for you. I haven't decided on the exact amount yet, but if from now on my sheep are safe, then you can rest assured that I shall reward you handsomely."

So the deal was struck and every night from dusk until dawn, Leopard could be seen taking up his position at the entrance to the farm. However, the very fact that he could be seen meant that Racoon and Rat decided to temporarily stop their killing spree. After all, there were other things they could eat and Leopard would eventually tire of his job. So they lay low and waited.

Realising that he needed to lay a trap for the two hungry animals, the shepherd decided to disguise Leopard as a sheep and the following night, Leopard wore a fleece.

Instead of keeping apart from the flock, he mingled with them, the better to fool whoever might be watching. Wearing two coats, his own and the fleece, Leopard looked extra fat and tempting, and so it was that when Racoon and Rat decided that the time was right to steal another innocent creature, they were easily lured into capturing him.

However, as Rat was taking his turn in carrying Leopard away, balanced on his head, he noticed whiskers and claws protruding from beneath the fleece which suddenly didn't seem to fit very well.

"Come and take your turn, Racoon. I cannot go another step with this heavy load. Just let me rest here a little and I will soon catch you up and be ready to help again," gasped Rat.

Leopard dressed in white fleece hiding amongst flock of sheep

It was not long before Racoon, too, was exhausted, and he was extremely relieved to see Rat rushing to rejoin him.Instead of taking over the heavy load, Rat began to sing:

My friend, Racoon, just drop your load.
My friend, Racoon, just drop your load.
Look at the whiskers, look at the claws,
Look at the mouth, the set of the jaws
My friend, Racoon, just drop your load.
Listen to me, just drop your load.

Listening intently and with fear clutching his heart, Racoon nevertheless managed to reply to Rat:

My old friend, Rat, I hear your words.
My old friend, Rat, I hear your words.
I'll finish the journey to my hole
Where I will drop it, so please be there.
My old friend, Rat, I'll drop my load.
Listen to me, you must be there.

As Racoon stumbled up to his hole, gasping for breath, he dropped Leopard and darted towards the tiny entrance, but before he could reach safety, Leopard stretched out his mighty paw and grabbed him. In an instant, Rat leaped up onto Leopard's back and bit him so hard that he lost his grip, yowling in pain.

Leopard is chasing Racoon while Rat bites his back.

In that brief instant, for brief instant it was, the two small animals made their escape, but if you have ever wondered why the racoon has a striped back, you have only to remember how sharp the leopard's claws are.

Storyteller: *An old lady told me this story on my way here to meet you*
Audience: *Is that so? Then long may your tongue be oiled.*
Storyteller: *And long may your ears be greased.*

Storytelling village: *Have.*